First U.S. edition 2008

Library of Congress Cataloging-in-Publication Data is available.

Library of Congress Catalog Card Number 2007052186

ISBN 978-0-7636-3856-6

2 4 6 8 10 9 7 5 3 1

Printed in Singapore

This book was typeset in Truesdell.
The illustrations were done in oil on paper.

Candlewick Press
2067 Massachusetts Avenue
Cambridge, Massachusetts 02140

visit us at www.candlewick.com

For Lily
M. E.

For Nora
N. S.

Cinderella

retold by Max Eilenberg

illustrated by

Niamh Sharkey

CANDLEWICK PRESS
CAMBRIDGE, MASSACHUSETTS

ONCE UPON A TIME there lived a girl whose mother — the kindest mother in all the world — had died and whose father had married again.

The wedding had barely ended before the new wife began to reveal her true nature. She was snobbish, mean, and foul-tempered. Ooh, she was horrid!

And she was especially cruel to the girl, whose beauty made her own two daughters look positively hideous. The stepmother couldn't stand this.

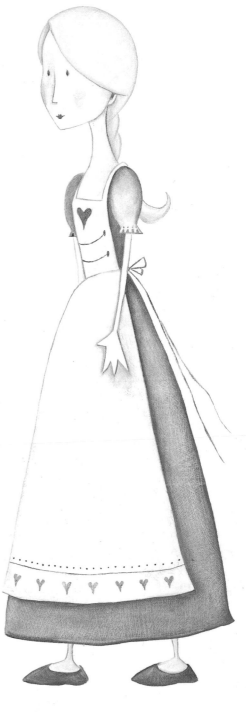

The girl's father never said a word.
He didn't seem to notice how unkind the
stepmother was or how she blamed the
girl for everything. It was as if he had
fallen completely under the woman's spell.

Poor girl!
Every day the
stepmother made
her work so hard:
cook, clean,
dust, sweep,
rub, scrub,
peel, polish,
from first thing in the
morning to last thing
at night, until her
arms ached and
her head spun.

The stepsisters didn't care.
They were as nasty as their mother.
They loved to watch the girl work.

Ooh, they loved it.

They lolled around.
They laughed at her.
They mocked her tattered rags.

At night they made her sleep
in the corner by the chimney,
among the cinders . . .

and they called her

Cinderella.

Now, it happened one day that the king decided to hold a great ball for his son, the prince. The stepmother made sure that her daughters were invited.

Invitation to a Ball
Friday 8 p.m.

The stepsisters spent the whole week shopping. They bought expensive outfits,  an enormous amount of jewelry, and some very large hats.

They thought they looked beautiful!
(In fact, they looked frightful.)

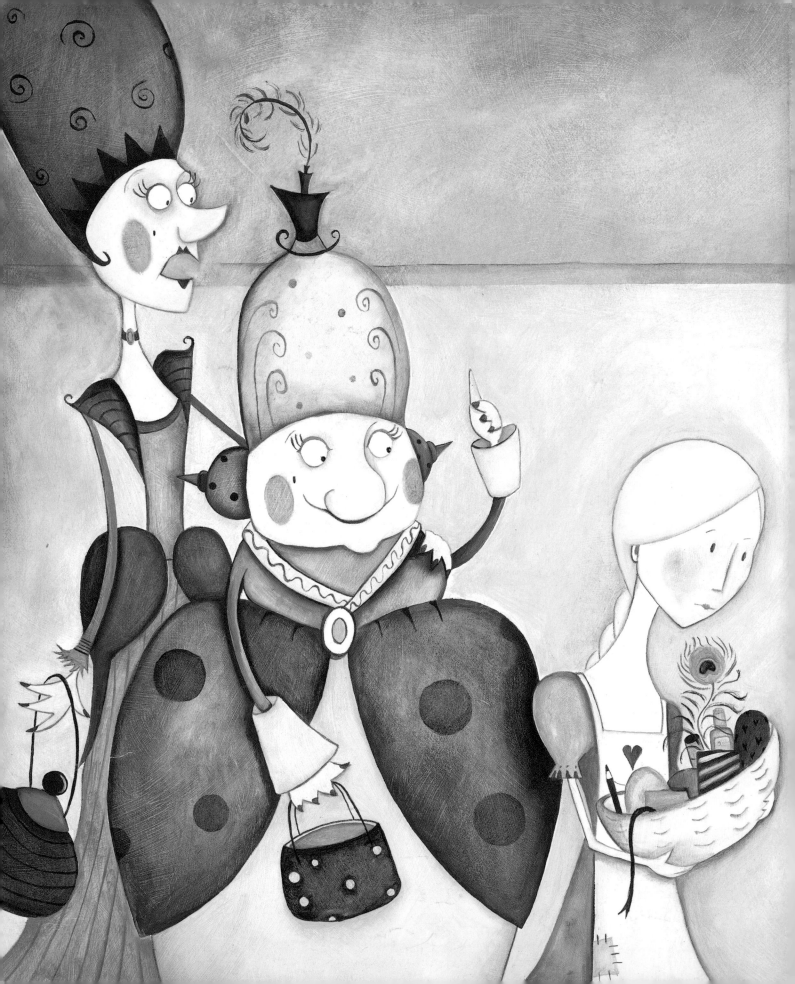

At last it was the day of the ball.
"I wish I could go," said Cinderella, who
had worked so hard to get her stepsisters ready.
"Well, you can't!" shouted the stepmother.
"No one cares about you! Get out your mop."
And off she went with her husband trailing
silently behind her.

Poor Cinderella was left all alone.
"I wish I could go to the ball," she sighed.

"And so you shall," said a pleasant voice.

Cinderella jumped up in surprise.

There before her was a small, kindly-
looking woman, hovering in the air and
holding a large silver wand. "Who are you?"
Cinderella said with a gasp.

"I'm your fairy godmother, dear.
Now, bring me a pumpkin
from the garden."

Cinderella had no idea how a pumpkin could help. But her fairy godmother simply tapped it with her wand.

Tap tap WHOOSH!

There stood a magnificent golden carriage. "Oh!" said Cinderella.

"Horses next," said the fairy godmother.
"We'll need some mice."

Tap *tap* went the wand. WHISH!

The mice turned into a splendid set of
horses, all a lovely dappled gray.

"Now for a coachman," said the fairy godmother, pointing to the rattrap. There were three fine rats. Cinderella chose the one with the longest whiskers.

KAPOUFF!

There stood a proud, stout coachman, with a most superior mustache!

"Footmen," said the fairy godmother. "Lizards, please."

KaPaFFF!

Two tall footmen climbed up behind the carriage in their smart tailcoats and silken top hats as if they'd done nothing else all their lives.

"That," said the fairy godmother,
"just leaves those rags."
Light sparkled from her wand.
"Oh!" said Cinderella. Her rags were gone.
In their place was a beautiful blue silk dress.
And there were pearls on her shoes and
sapphires in her hair! She could hardly
believe her eyes.

"Have a lovely time at the ball," said the
fairy godmother, "but do not stay past
midnight, or all your magic will be lost."

"I promise!" said Cinderella.
And off she went.

At the palace, the ball had already begun, and music and laughter filled the air.

But when Cinderella arrived, everyone stopped.

She was so beautiful!

Nobody knew who she was, not even her stepsisters. The prince came to greet her, thinking she must be a grand princess. He asked her to dance. They danced again . . . and again!

Cinderella could not have been happier. But she remembered her promise and, at a quarter to midnight, slipped quietly away.

When the prince saw that she was gone, he was miserable. He asked everyone her name — but nobody knew who she was.

The very next morning, the king announced that there would be another ball, for his son longed to see the beautiful princess again.

The stepsisters spent the whole week taking
dancing lessons.
(They were useless.)
They spent a fortune on blue silk dresses.
(They still looked frightful.)

At last came the day of the ball.

"I wish I could go," said Cinderella,
who had dreamed of the
handsome prince every night.

"Be quiet!" shouted the
stepmother. "Get back to your
work!" And off they all went
without Cinderella, slamming
the door behind them.

Cinderella sighed.

"Maybe I can help, dear," said a familiar voice.

It was the fairy godmother!

She waved her wand. The pumpkin carriage and its horses appeared, with the coachman and footmen all aboard.

Then suddenly Cinderella's rags were gone and she was wearing a dress of shimmering silver. Her shoes and her hair sparkled with diamonds. She could never have imagined anything so lovely.

The fairy godmother smiled. "Your carriage awaits," she said. "But remember to be home before midnight."

"I promise," said Cinderella happily.

At the palace, Cinderella outshone everyone. All the fine ladies wore blue, but her silver dress made them look ordinary.

The prince's heart leaped as he ran to take her hand. She was even lovelier than he remembered.

Then he led her to the dance floor.

How beautifully they danced together! Cinderella was so lost in happiness that she almost forgot the time. It was very nearly midnight before she remembered her promise and quietly slipped away.

The prince ran after her, but she was already gone. He returned to the palace full of longing, for she had stolen his heart.

The following morning, the king announced that there would be another ball that very night, for his son was too much in love to wait any longer.

The stepsisters ordered silver dresses and diamonds. Cinderella worked hard all day to make them beautiful. (It simply wasn't possible.)

Then at last it was time to go. "I wish—" said Cinderella.

"Well, don't!" shouted the stepmother. And off they all went without Cinderella, slamming the door behind them.

Poor Cinderella — how she longed to see her prince!

"Don't worry, dear," said the kindly voice.
It was the fairy godmother again!
She waved her wand. The pumpkin carriage and its horses appeared, with the coachman and footmen standing ready.

Then Cinderella's rags were gone. Instead she wore a gown of pure, bright gold. And on her feet were slippers made of glass — the finest, most magical shoes in the world.

"Perfect," said the fairy godmother. "Now, don't forget to be back before midnight."

"I promise," said Cinderella.

At the palace, Cinderella dazzled everyone. All the fine ladies wore silver now, but her golden dress made them look dull. The prince was more in love than ever. He took her hand and they danced. They danced the whole evening, blissfully happy. Time melted away.

Cinderella didn't notice the hours passing, until suddenly — BONG — the clock started striking midnight.

BONG

BONG BONG

BONG BONG

OH, NO!

BONG
BONG
BONG
BONG
BONG

RUN, CINDERELLA, RUN!
RUN, RUN, RUN!

As she fled, her shoe fell off,
but she dared not stop to pick it up.

BONGGG!

The prince ran out after her, but
she was gone. All that remained
was a precious glass slipper.

The next morning the prince announced
that he would marry the girl whose
foot fitted the slipper.

Then he set out to find her.

The prince traveled the kingdom, stopping
at every house.

Every girl he met tried the slipper on,
for every girl wanted to marry the prince.

But the slipper fitted none of them.
The prince kept looking.

At last he came to the stepmother's house. "Meet my daughters," she said, rubbing her hands with glee.

Well, the stepsisters tried. They pinched and pushed, they squeezed and shoved — but they couldn't make the slipper fit. The stepmother was furious.

"Is there no one else?" the prince said with a sigh.

"No, there isn't," the stepmother snapped.

"Yes, there *is*," said a voice Cinderella had almost forgotten. Surely it couldn't be. She hardly dared to believe it.

Her father! It was as if he had woken from a deep sleep. He turned toward her and smiled. "There's my daughter," he said.

Cinderella stepped forward from the shadows, her heart beating quickly. "May I try the slipper?" she asked.

The prince looked closely at her face. Then, carefully, gently, he knelt down and held out the glass slipper.

It fitted perfectly!

"It's you!" cried the prince, taking Cinderella in his arms and kissing her. "You are my love!"

"At last!" said another voice. There was the fairy godmother. She waved her wand, and once more Cinderella's rags were transformed.

Very soon afterward Cinderella and the prince were married. Cinderella's father scattered flowers, and the king led the cheers. The stepmother and stepsisters did their best to look pleased. (They didn't quite manage it.)

As for Cinderella, her wishes had all come true. She loved her prince, and her prince loved her. And that's the way it was,

forever after.